The Magic of Little Bear

THE MIDDLE CHILD

BoAnn

Balboa Press books may be ordered through booksellers or by contacting:

Balboa Press
A Division of Hay House
1663 Liberty Drive
Bloomington, IN 47403
www.balboapress.com
1 (877) 407-4847

Because of the dynamic nature of the Internet, any web addresses or links contained in this book may have changed
since publication and may no longer be valid. The views expressed in this work are solely those of the author and do
not necessarily reflect the views of the publisher, and the publisher hereby disclaims any responsibility for them.

Any people depicted in stock imagery provided by Getty Images are models,
and such images are being used for illustrative purposes only.
Certain stock imagery © Getty Images.

ISBN: 978-1-9822-0480-8 (sc)
ISBN: 978-1-9822-0481-5 (e)

Library of Congress Control Number: 2018906238

Print information available on the last page.

Balboa Press rev. date: 05/25/2018

BALBOA
PRESS
A DIVISION OF HAY HOUSE

*Dedicated to our children and
our first grandchild!*

Welcome!

Yes, welcome… to a magical adventure that proves that everything is possible and that will give you a new outlook on the present. I will take you along for the ride to amazing fairy-tale places, both in the past and in the now. You'll experience familiar and new things and you'll discover how you can use magic in those situations to make your life that much happier.

All is well. When you're happy, everything just feels easier and all your dreams can come true. Oh, isn't that a great thought? Dreams coming true? They can! You see, we're here to enjoy our lives as if it's an endless holiday of fun filled days and great adventures. All those adventures, big and small, will help you grow. I'm here to guide you and… to wish you a happy holiday!

Come with me, it's time to start! Let me tell you everything…

The middle child

Saskia is a sweet girl, a little quiet and ten years old. She usually wears her blonde hair in a ponytail, which her mother fixes for her every morning. When daddy does it, Saskia doesn't really like it, because he puts the ponytail right on top of her head! Dad likes her hair that way, but she thinks it looks silly. Saskia has one older sister, Kristien, who's always getting up to mischief. Kristien already goes to high school and she's very busy and talkative. Piet is Saskia's younger brother. He just turned one year old, so he's still in diapers and is learning how to walk. Saskia and her family live in a terraced house in a lovely little village in Frisia. She likes to play in their garden; a big field surrounded by trees and a small stream with a wooden board going across it. In the meadow on the other side are two beautiful horses, whinnying and grazing contently.

Saskia is sitting on the swing made by her dad. He is quite the handyman; he also built a sandbox and the rabbit home where her rabbit Pluisje lives. He was a birthday present and she has to take care of him, of course. Pluisje is a very fluffy rabbit, so that's where his name came from. Saskia watches the horses, standing next to each other, and a little farther away is the farm of farmer De Vries. There are several black-and-white cows in the field next to it. Just behind the farm is the dike, with the sea behind it, which you can smell all day long. Sometimes Saskia goes there with Neighbour to scout for things that washed ashore. He is a beachcomber, and he takes all kinds of things home with him. They always find something. Boards, for instance, that Neighbour gave to dad to build Pluisjes home with. Saskia likes searching for feathers of seabirds, her collection is quite big, and one day they found a buoy and a plastic bottle with a note inside. A message in a bottle! Saskia and Neighbour once sent a note that way, out to sea, for someone else to find. "Sas," mom calls, "Dinner!" "I'm coming, mom!" Saskia replies from the garden. Saskia goes inside and sits down at the dinner table. Her brother Piet is already in his high chair and Kristien is talking nineteen to the dozen again. She's talking about school and annoying teachers, who mess things up. Dad is nodding every now and again.'My teacher is kind of nice.' Saskia thinks, and she watches her family quietly. Mom gives her a dinner plate and says: "Enjoy your meal." Saskia looks at her dinner dish. Spinach, yuck. Kristien is talking to dad, and mom talks to little Piet, who gibbers back between the spoonsful mom is feeding him. He is messing with his food, so slowly but steadily everything turns green from the spinach. Saskia watches them, slowly eating her own dinner.

"Dad, Pluisjes home needs to be cleaned." she says, but dad doesn't hear her, because Kristien keeps on chatting. "Mom?" she asks, but her mother is busy with little Piet, who has the spinach in his hair and on his face now. Saskia eats her spinach, but she's trifling with her food. Somehow the spinach is hard to swallow."Carry on, I've got more to do today." mom complains, looking at her. Mom and dad are very sweet, but they're always busy. "Oh, mom, Pluisjes house needs…" Saskia starts, but mom interrupts her."Not now, Sas, finish your dinner and go play."Piet is green all over now, jeez… Kristien is still in deep conversation with dad about school and all kinds of topics. Saskia empties her plate, stands up and walks to the backdoor. At the table everything carries on as if she was never there, nobody seems to miss her. Her sister jabbers on and on and mom tries to keep the parts of Piet that aren't green yet clean. In the garden Saskia starts talking to Pluisje, whose red eyes watch her, his little ears hanging down his cheeks. He's nibbling on a carrot dad gave Sas to feed him, listening to her soft voice.

"Hey Pluisje. How's your carrot? You're never busy, are you? Me neither. You can hear me, can't you? Do you want some more grass?"She sighs. Behind Saskia a horse whinnies: "Heaaeaabrrrrrrbrrrrbru!" That means he's happy. The wind is blowing in the garden, causing the leaves in the chestnut tree to rustle, and the reeds in the stream are making their own kind of music. Swallows go 'sweet, sweet' in the sky and if she listens very closely, Saskia can hear the waves breaking on the boulders. The lovely sounds of nature.

Sleeping

Saskia is lying in her bed, the bed that dad made for her. It's right under the slanted roof, beneath the big window. Mom always closes the curtains, but when she's gone, Saskia opens them again so she can see the sunset. With the blankets all the way up to her chin she watches the moon and the stars. Blue light sparkles around her little bedroom and everything becomes magic in the moonlight, different somehow. Her toys and schoolbooks, even the walls are different. It's a beautiful night, with lots of stars. Saskia watches the Big Dipper; the Big Bear. Daddy taught her that. It doesn't look like a bear, but rather like the saucepan that mom has in her cupboard. "Good evening, Big Bear, good evening, moon." Saskia says softly."Can you tell me why everyone is so busy all the time? Why doesn't anyone ever listen to me? Pluisjes home really needs to be cleaned… Why isn't Kristien ever nice to me and why am I so alone?"Saskia doesn't understand, she doesn't get people, why they do the things they do. Saskia is a thinker. She's always thinking things over and trying to understand everything. Silently she lies there in her warm bed, looking up at the starry night that slowly passes by her window. Her eyes start to close. "I wish everything was different." she thinks and before she falls asleep, a last little twinkle passes through the stars of the Big Bear. "What could that be?" she wonders, but then she drifts off to dreamland.

Little Bear

Somewhere, I don't know where exactly, Little Bear starts to feel something. At the precise moment the stars of the Big Bear twinkle, Little Bears tummy lights up, just for a second, and he knows exactly where he needs to be.

The next day

Friday. Off to school. Today is an exciting day because it's report card day. It's the last day of school, so everyone will get their report cards and then the summer holidays start! Saskia is at the breakfast table eating a sandwich. Kirstien is already on her way for a while, with the bus to High School with the annoying teachers. Dad is also already gone, off to work. Little Piet is in his high chair nibbling on some bread. Mom is busy, getting everything ready to bring Piet to daycare. "Mom, Pluisjes home needs…" "Yeah, yeah, I know. I'll ask dad tomorrow, but now I have to go, sweetie.""Okay." Saskia says and she finishes her sandwich. "Mom, I'm done, I'm going to school now, see you this afternoon!"Saskia drinks the rest of her milk, picks up her lunch box and walks toward the door."Bye Sas, see you later. Do keep on walking, okay? No dawdling, otherwise you'll be late again."

Saskia strolls through the little streets to school at the edge of the village. She gets on the swings at the playground for a bit, picks a beautiful flower and pets the dog of Rugged Cees, who shows up, barking loudly. He is always barking and jumping, so Saskia named him Barking Dog. Report card day; Saskia is looking forward to it, but she's also a little apprehensive. She is in group 7, but she's a slow learner. She's often daydreaming during class and although she can hear her teacher talk, her mind tends to wander to other things. The bell rings and Saskia starts running to arrive just in time! It's crowded on the schoolyard, the little kids have already entered the school and Saskia enters as one of the last through the big wooden doors. Everyone talks and runs to their classrooms to find their seats. Saskia's seat is next to the window, with two desks in front of her and two behind her. On the other side of the classroom is a bookcase. In the corner of the bookcase is a little bear, that Saskia has never seen before and above it are posters of birds and countries. Saskia's teacher is standing in front of the class with a desk behind her. She's in front of the big digiboard on which is written 'report cards' in big, elegant letters. School. It has its own scents. The scent of paint and glue of the craftworks they made yesterday, the flowers in the windowsill, the scent of books and the sweaty feet of Hendrik, ew! "We're going to start…" the teacher calls over the noise and slowly it gets quiet. The teacher starts explaining what they're going to do today, what will happen in the morning, until break. First regular schoolwork and then the report cards. Teacher starts with geography. She points at the big map of Europe and starts calling out the countries. Saskia stares out of the window, to the trees, the farm and the cows in the meadow of farmer De Vries. "Weird cows…" she thinks. "Eating all day… lying down… strolling through the meadow. Look at it, that one cow is eating grass next to a cow pie, ew! I'd rather have spinach."

"Saskia van der Vlucht! Pay attention, girl, what did I just say? Well?" Saskia doesn't know and she feels herself going red. "Why do I have to know all that?" she thinks. "Dad had an atlas and if I want to know which country is which, I can just check it out.""Now pay attention!" the teacher says and Saskia nods. She looks at the map attentively. Norway, Sweden, Finland… The long stick taps the map. Iceland is a funny country, it's like a little green dot in the blue, haha. Ringgggg! Break, finally.Everyone runs around on the schoolyard, playing games, like jump rope and playing with marbles, but also gossiping and giggling. The boys are with the boys and the girls with the girls.Saskia doesn't really play along, she's mostly alone, strolling around. Everyone is already playing with someone, so she walks towards the swings and watches the cows. The teacher is smoking a cigarette, how disgusting. When she's finished with it, she smells even worse than Smelly-feet Hendrik!

"Hello Saskia," Smelly-feet Hendrik says. He is on the other swing. "Do you think you will pass?"Hendrik is a slow learner as well and he too is daydreaming a lot of the time. That's how the teacher calls it. Hendriks mother passed away. In the churchyard in the village is a tombstone with her name on it; she is buried there. Saskia shudders to think about it, how horrible. But it happened and Hendrik was very sad, but now he's doing a lot better. He changed, though. He is different now. He became more quiet and a lot less happy than he used to be. Would he be okay?Hendrik was more quiet than usual today. Saskia thinks he's a little scared. "I hope so," she answers, "I did my very best. Stupid math is so difficult."Hendrik stays quiet, almost everything is difficult for him. Sometimes he gets bullied, but Saskia never does that! It's so stupid and unfair. Luckily it doesn't happen all the time, because at gym class he's the best and the fastest. And he even surprises the teacher with his amazing drawings. Sometimes she puts one of his drawings on display for everyone to see and then he's very proud. It changes him. He looks different when that happens; his eyes start to sparkle."I wonder if he'll pass." Saskia thinks. "I sure hope so."

When the bell rings a little while later, everyone goes back to the classroom and sits down again. When they all found their seats, Saskia can feel the tension. It's quiet a little too fast. On the teachers desk is a pile of blue folders. The teacher is talking about everything they did this year, all the things they've learned and then she starts calling out names alphabetically. The person who's name is called, has to walk to the front of the class to receive his or her report card and the teacher says something about every one of them. When your last name is Van der Vlucht, it takes a while to get there. Hmm…It's Hendriks turn.

"Hendrik," the teacher says, "You've been working very hard this year and your grades went up quite a lot!" Hendrik looks happy. "But I want to talk to you later, okay?" Now Hendrik isn't smiling anymore. He is looking at the teacher with big eyes while she gives him his report card. "It'll be okay. Go sit down." the teacher says softly. "Hendrik is being held back a year!" someone from the back of the class calls out. It sounds shrill and harsh. A few kids that already received their report cards start to snigger. "Quiet!" The teacher yells and she continues handing out the report cards. Hendrik quickly slides back onto his chair, his report card clenched in his hand so hard that his knuckles turned white. His face is pale and white. Next are Els and Erik and then, finally, it's Saskia's turn to go to the front of the class. "Saskia!" the teacher calls out. She walks toward her and looks up hopefully. "Saskia, you have a nice report card. Carry on like this and you'll get there.""Thank you, miss." Saskia replies and she returns to her desk. *'You'll get there.'* Mom uses that phrase sometimes, but where it is you'll be getting? Saskia asked dad once, but he didn't answer. He had laughed and called her a wiseguy. Weird."Chris…" the teacher says.After a while everyone has their report cards, the result of a whole schoolyear. The morning is over and the summer holiday starts.Saskia's classmates leave the classroom, shouting, laughing and running, through the gate and off to their homes. They all walk past her. Saskia turns around and sees Hendrik and the teacher through the window. Hendrik is looking down and the teacher has her hand on his shoulder. Saskia feels sorry for Hendrik. She just can't understand why other kids would laugh at that, at him. "What would the teacher be telling Hendrik?" Saskia thinks. "I'm going to ask him later…"

On the way home, the holiday started

Saskia is walking home through the little streets, between big and small houses along the neatly trimmed hedges. Along the way she meets Barking Dog again, standing next to Rugged Cees."Watch out for Rugged Cees!" Saskia hears her mother say, but she doesn't really understand why mom says that. Rugged Cees is a little odd looking; his hair is always on end. He talks with an accent and he is from the big city so he doesn't really fit in. He lives in a little cottage on the other side of the village. It's crooked and definitely needs a paintjob. Rugged Cees' garden is a mess, overgrown with weeds and flowers. There is a white goat in the front yard, always bleating and it's sometimes standing right on top of his little wooden home. There is also a pony, that Rugged Cees lets inside his house sometimes, chickens and a few cats. He lives there alone with all his animals. When Barking Dog spots her, he runs towards her and starts jumping around, wagging his tail. Saskia pets him. "Hi, Barking Dog." she says.Rugged Cees comes over. "I can't believe this," he says in his city-accent. "He's from the animal shelter and usually he's scared of everything and everyone, especially kids." He looks at her. "You must be a special kid, for him to behave this way, there's no doubt about it."Saskia strokes the soft fur. "What's his name?""Erm… Just 'Dog'. Come Dog, let's go."Barking Dog follows his master, looks around a few times and, still barking, keeps on trotting next to Rugged Cees, who shakes his head.

"A special kid…" Saskia hears him say. "A special kid, right, Dog?" Barking Dog barks happily, he agrees with his master. The dog looks at Saskia one last time, who is on her way home again, and runs to a tree along the road. He stops and starts barking at the tree. "Come." Rugged Cees says. "Bye, bear." Barking Dog thinks and he barks one last time to a little bear that is sitting high up in the tree, between the leafs. "Weird Cees." Saskia thinks, walking. She reaches the little playground and the swings are free. Time for a bit of swinging! Sitting on the swing, she removes her report card from the shining folder, opens it and goes to the very last page. Group 7, the last column: reading and writing 6, math 5,5, world orientation 6,5 and, hey, English an 8!

Happily Saskia puts away her report card. She never received an 8 before, yes! She jumps off the swing and skips home. The church bells toll; it's noon.

Home

"Mom, I got an 8!" Saskia calls out, entering the garden. The back door is locked, mom isn't home yet. She's fetching little Piet from daycare, sometimes that takes a little longer than expected. The key to the back door is under the flowerpot and quickly Saskia enters the house. There is mom already, she just got little Piet from the car. Saskia opens the front door for her. "I've got an 8 for English, mom!" Saskia squeals and she skips around. "Weekend." mom calls out. Little Piet is struggling and gibbering in her arms, he wants to walk around, so mom puts him down. "Tep, tep, tep, Piet tep!" he yells. A little wobbly he starts stepping around, falls over a few times and starts playing with a ball in his playing corner. He's sitting down now, safely on his big diaper. "Mom, I've got an 8 for English!" Saskia calls out again, waving her report card around. "That's great, girl, you're doing well. Shall we take a look at your report card tonight, I've got a lot to do now. Can you watch Piet for a bit?" "Alright, mom." Saskia answers crestfallen, her hand slumping down her side. Mom is already doing all kinds of chores, like mothers do. "What do you want on your sandwich?" mom asks from the kitchen. "Peanut butter?"A little while later Saskia is sitting on the couch with her peanut butter sandwich, watching her little brother. Mom is upstairs, turning on the washing machine or something. A little sad Saskia takes a bite from the sandwich mom hastily gave her. Her 8 suddenly isn't that important anymore, mom is so busy. "I'm not that good anyway." Saskia sighs, quietly eating her sandwich.

Later that afternoon she's in the garden while little Piet takes his nap and mom is vacuuming. "Hello Pluisje, I've got an 8 for English, isn't that great?" Pluisje watches her with his smart red eyes and slowly his little head goes from left to right. In the corner of his home is a big triangle of droppings. All the way up in the tree is Little Bear on a branch, rocking back and forth in the wind and watching Saskia on the floor next to the rabbit home. With his clever beady eyes he watches her and with his small ears he hears what she says and thinks. Saskia plays away the afternoon until dad comes home. She tries to tell him about her 8, but he has to take a shower and get dressed. Then Kristien comes along, all happy and chatting. She also received her report card today, but her summer holidays already started a week ago. During dinner Saskia tries to tell everyone about her grades, but Kristien is talking again and her grades are a lot better than Saskia's. She jabbers on about exams, tests and teachers. Saskia is happy for Kristien, of course, but she thinks it's a little weird; Saskia only has one teacher, not multiple. Mom and dad are also happy for Kristien and tell her all the things she can become with such good grades. Mom is busy tending to Piet, while Saskia quietly eats her dinner. The table is cleared and Piet is brought upstairs, to bed. That evening they're all on the couch watching tv. Mom, dad and Kristien are talking, but Saskia is watching the tv with her thumb in her mouth. She is a little too old for that, but sometimes she does it until mom notices. At half past eight it's Saskia's bedtime and mom brings her upstairs. "Goodnight, Sas." she says, closing the curtains. Saskia looks at her cupboard. Standing upright against the wall is her very first 8, that nobody got to see. She hears the voices downstairs and her dads laughter. Saskia is sad. Why is she so dumb, why isn't she a little more like Kristien? She wished that she could learn so easily and was doing as well in school. Nobody notices her, not at school, not at home, only sweet, sweet Pluisje does...Slowly the sun sets. Saskia opens the curtains and sees the first star appear. It becomes a blur through her tears. Quickly she dries her eyes on the bedsheets. The moon appears from behind a tree and blue light bounces around her bedroom. The Big Dipper, the Big Bear, becomes visible, and next is the polar star in the Little Bear. Dad told her about it a long time ago, he knows a lot about stars, but he doesn't have time for Saskia anymore nowadays. "That's okay," Saskia thinks sadly, "I can't do a lot anyway." The stars twinkle softly. It's a bright night and the blue light shines right on her report card. Slowly Saskia starts to drift off. Next to the report card is a Little Bear, she can see him. It looks like he's shining as well, twinkling, like the stars. Already half asleep Saskia thinks: "He was there at school today, in the bookcase... How did he get here?" Saskia's eyes close and she's off to dreamland, dreaming about bears, stars and rabbits...

Saskia wakes up

The sun is shining in Saskia's bedroom. It's already daylight and she's awake, but she's still cosy in her bed. "The summer holidays," she thinks, "Six weeks, that's almost forever!" The house is silent. Her alarm tells her it's seven o clock. It's Saturday, so everyone is still asleep, even little Piet isn't making a sound. Saskia opens the big window and crawls back into her warm bed. A soft breeze flows over her face and brings the lovely scents from outside. Her arms are above the covers, tickling her bare skin, it feels like the wind wants to take her away. Saskia thinks about yesterday; about her report card, her 8 and about poor Hendrik who always smells a bit. His father probably doesn't tell him to shower every day. His mother is gone. She died of a terrible illness, only two years ago. From that moment on Hendrik changed, he became quiet and withdrawn. Saskia hopes he won't be held back, because she actually likes him a lot. He's nice. She smiles thinking about Hendrik. He'll be okay...

Little Bear

Little Bear is listening to Saskia's thoughts. He is magic, so he can do that. His little face curls into a smile; sweet Saskia isn't worried about Hendrik. "That's good," he thinks, "Worrying means seeing problems that aren't there yet." He had discovered that when he was wandering around the forests with Angelo, a long time ago, when they discovered the magic.

I will tell you more about Angelo later...

Little Bear is looking at Saskia, in her bed, eyes closed, taking in the scents from outside. He stands up, walks toward the report card and places it face down in the cupboard.

Saskia discovers Little Bear

Suddenly Saskia remembers seeing Little Bear sitting on her cupboard when she was falling asleep. She sits bolt upright and looks at the cupboard; no bear. Huh, he's sitting on the other side now, right on top of her report card, that she had definitely put upright on the shelf! It's the same bear as at school, how did he get here? She gets out of bed, walks over to the cupboard and picks up the bear. He is old, his eyes look like little pebbles and his fur is a mishmash of materials. He's also a bit dirty... "How did he get here?" she thinks and at that moment she hears a voice in her head say: "Hello, Saskia." Saskia gives a yelp of fright, throws the bear on her cupboard and jumps on her bed. What was that? "Don't be frightened," she hears inside her head, "It's okay.

You asked for something and sometimes you get something back, and sometimes that something is me. Don't be scared, it's alright." Saskia stays quiet. "What is this?" she thinks. "Am I still dreaming?" She pinches her arm. "Ouch!" Not dreaming then. She looks at Little Bear, lying in the cupboard on his side, facing the wall. Light is coming from Little Bear and he moves. Saskia crawls under the covers, pulls them over her head, but still she keeps watching curiously. Little Bear starts to change. He sits up against the wall, watching Saskia with his pebble-eyes suddenly alive, his fur shiny and sleek. "Hello Saskia," Little Bear says. From underneath the covers with only the top of her head sticking out she looks at something that simply can't be! She's not dreaming because she hears little Piet cooing and mom getting up to fetch him. "Who... what are you?" Saskia stammers. "I am Little Bear," Little Bear answers. "I was made by Angelo, a long time ago, out of stardust from the Starry Sky. The same stars you were watching last night, the ones your dad told you about. I am here because you have a lot of questions. Your question is floating around and then the answer comes to you;

something starts to appear in your life. That's how it works. Everything you ask always comes to you, every time, and now I am here for you. I heard your questions. The magic of the earth, the sun, the moon, the stars and everything in between brought us together." Little Bear falls silent and looks at Saskia, who is still watching him from under the blankets. "Yes, who or what I am… Angelo made me a long, long, long time ago. It was in a country where very little people lived, not as many as now, and he lived near the river. He lived on the same earth you walk on now, but it was very different. It was a younger earth with a younger sun. The trees grew higher and the leaves were greener. Everywhere there were beautiful flowers in every colour imaginable. The young sun, that sometimes couldn't even penetrate the thick canopy, let everything bathe in a fairy-tale-like glow. There were birds and butterflies, some very big, and every now and then a fairy would flutter by, going somewhere we don't know… It was a magical world.

You can still see the magic in everything around you. But listen, what I'm about to tell you will surprise you: the magic is just as strong now as it was back then, if you only look and listen very carefully! It seems like people lost the magic, they don't believe anymore. Most people would want to believe, but they have been told magic doesn't exist, that it's all imagination. But slowly it's starting to come back, some start to discover the magic again, they start to wonder again. They stand still and are amazed." Saskia stays safely under the covers and looks at the bear in her cupboard. He looks beautiful now, with shining eyes, but he is still and silent. She watches him for a while. "This is impossible," she thinks, "and yet there is a bear there, ugly and dirty at first, but now kind of pretty. He isn't moving now. Did I dream this after all? He was at the cupboard at school before, but now he's here, how can that be? He says he is made by Angelo, but who is Angelo? Magic? Fairies? I don't understand…" Saskia hears mom going downstairs with a gleefully squealing Piet. "Mom! Come quick! There's a bear in my room and it's talking to me!" She hears her mother stop walking down the stairs, turn around, and a moment later she's standing in Saskia's room. "What did you say?" mom asks, putting Piet down, "A bear that's talking to you? You've been dreaming, sweetie. There's no such thing as talking bears, not even in the circus. Where is it?" From underneath the blankets a small hand appears, pointing at the cupboard. Mom turns around and sees the bear. "Ha, that's cute. Where did you get it? It's a little old and dusty though." Mom picks up the bear and dusts it off a bit. "Did you find it somewhere?" She looks at the bear from all sides, pats him a few times and puts him back. "Ouch! Take it easy! Jeez, my butt." Little Bear thinks, but he stays still. Adults… That's a whole other story. "You dreamed it all, honey. It's just a teddy bear and he's a little frayed. Look, the stuffing is poking out of the seams. I'll fix him for you later." Saskia pulls back the covers. "That's weird," she thinks, "Mom sees an old bear, but I see something else…" She gets out of bed and walks to the cupboard. "Have I been dreaming after all? I don't see any stuffing sticking out anywhere." The bear has lovely shining fur and twinkling eyes. Saskia doesn't get it, but it excites her at the same time. "It's weird." she says out loud. "Just a dream," mom says and she picks up little Piet. "Come Piet, time for a new diaper. Do you want a nice fresh oven baked bun?" Mom leaves the room. Saskia hears her go downstairs and she carefully pokes with her finger in the bears belly. "Teehee!" Little Bear says, "That tickles!" In a flash Saskia is on her bed. Dreaming, no way! Little Bear rubs his belly. "I'm very ticklish! And your mother hit me kind of hard." He rubs his backside. "Jeez, I'm not thát dusty!" From the bed Saskia watches the bear with her eyes wide. "What is your name?" she asks softly. "Little Bear," he answers. It's definitely not a dream then, so Saskia steps off the bed. Slowly she walks to the cupboard where Little Bear is walking around on the shelf. It looks like he is singing a song, but she can't make out the words. She smiles; it looks very funny. He's hobbling around on his stocky little legs. Saskia isn't scared anymore, only a little bit. He looks so cute! Just when she thinks that, he stops wiggling and looks at her. "So you're not afraid anymore. That's a good thing, Sas." "Why are you here?" Saskia asks.

Little Bear tells

Little Bear starts explaining. "Did I mention: because you asked? So here I am. You can ask me anything and I will answer. That's what you wanted, so that's what you get. Why isn't anyone listening to you, you asked, why isn't anyone playing with you? Why are you being teased sometimes and why does Kristien hurt you? Why are your mom and dad so busy, why don't they have time for you? Why are you thinking about Hendrik and pitying him? Why do people think Rugged Cees is weird, why is Barking Dog afraid of everything except you? I can continue for a while. What *I* would like to know is why you think you're stupid and why everyone and everything is more important than you are?" When Little Bear is talking his lips move a little but Saskia mainly hears his voice in her head. That's kind of odd. "Sas, I've got yummy buns!" mom calls from downstairs. Your mother is very sweet. You asks why she gives you so little attention, but she makes you fresh buns and yesterday she bought you a lollipop." "Hey," Saskia thinks, "That's true. And a while ago she got me a new doll and it wasn't even my birthday." "Look." Little Bear says, and he draws a circle in the air with his paw. All kind of twinkling things shoot from it. It's the Little Stars, the stardust of big Mister Bear and little Miss Bear. In a flash Saskia sees things in her head. She sees her mother teaching her how to ride a bike, putting a band-aid on her knee at the playground and pushing her on the swings. She sees mom building a sandcastle with her on the beach, making sandwiches for school with surprises inside, sometimes a little note or candy. And how she watches Saskia when she's asleep. Saskia didn't know that, but that's logical because she is asleep, so her eyes are closed. Saskia sees her mother watching her, in the images, watching only her with a beautiful smile and pure love in her eyes. Her hand goes through Saskia's hair and mom whispers: "My beautiful Sas." The twinkling shoots back into Little Bears paw and he looks at Saskia, standing there with big eyes of amazement. "What do you want to see? It's a choice and that's how it is. What you think about, the things you ask, will come to you. That part you will see and experience." Little Bear says. "You see your mom always working, always busy, and it seems to you that she doesn't have time for you. Because the magic always works, you get to see what you ask. Now you have a different picture. Try to hold on to that and let the magic work. Come. Let's go downstairs, you have a nice bun to eat!" He jumps into her arms. Saskia starts, but Little Bear feels nice and soft and, oddly enough, warm. Saskia can barely comprehend what is happening, but the nice images stay in her head. Holding Little Bear closely she walks downstairs.

The day begins

"Hi, Sas!" mom says. "Goodmorning, pretty girl." The table is set, there are warm buns in a basket and there are freshly picked flowers in a vase on the table. Little Piet is sitting in his high chair, washed and holding one of the white buns with lots of butter and chocolate sprinkles. He has some chocolate sprinkles on his face and he smells like baby.

"Goodmorning, mom." Saskia says and she puts Little Bear on the chair next to her. Dad is still sleeping. When Kristien doesn't have school, she always sleeps in as well, sometimes until noon! Mom sits down. "Did you recover from your bad dream?"

Saskia looks around the kitchen and then at her mother. She looks at her mom as if she sees her for the first time. The way her hair falls, her eyes, big and blue and her smiling mouth. "Yeah, mom, it was a weird dream." She takes a bun, puts on a lot of butter and also buries it with chocolate sprinkles. "Yummy, mom!" she says and she smiles widely at her mother. "Sweetie." her mom says. Little Piet coos: "Da, da, that." and he points his tiny finger at Saskia. "Akia, Assskia, that, that." They start laughing and talking together and finally Saskia tells mom about the eight for English on her report card. "Go get it," mom yells gleefully, "I want to see it!" Little Bear watches Saskia and mom and he is satisfied. He thinks about long ago when he was in the woods with Angelo and they discovered the fact that happiness creates happiness. Happiness wants to be where happiness is, so being happy means that happiness will come to you. Angelo was Little Bears mother and father simultaneously, if you think about it, because Angelo made him. Angelo, born in that world so long ago, had no siblings and he lived together with his mother in the forest. He grew up there. His mother was a herbalist and she knew everything there is to know about the forest, what lived and grew there. Angelo's father was a hunter who travelled the world. But when his dad was at home he used to tell the most wonderful stories by the campfire. Those were the best moments Angelo remembered. That's why he knew so much about the world, the forest and how you can live in harmony with nature and one day Angelo went his own way.

Dad comes downstairs as well and has breakfast with them. He looks at Saskia's other grades a little troubled. "Those need to be a little higher, lady." Saskia nods. He pours himself a cup of coffee and almost sits down on Little Bear. "What's this?" he asks as he picks him up by his thumb and forefinger. "Yuck, what is this filthy thing?" "Huh... What is up with that?" Saskia thinks, but in her head she hears Little Bears voice answer: "They can't see me like you can. To them

I am a dirty old bear, to you I am like you see me." Quickly Saskia looks at her parents, but they didn't hear anything. Mom says: "I'll fix that little bear with a needle and thread later and I'll put him in the washing machine."

Little Bear jumps up and down startled. "I don't want that!" it sounds in Saskia's head. "Do something! I don't want a needle and I don't want to go into the washing machine!" "Mom, it's okay." Saskia says quickly, "I like it the way it is." She laughs. "What's so funny?" dad asks. "Oh, nothing… heehee…" Saskia giggles.

A while later Saskia is in the garden, where she loves to be. Of course is Little Bear with her. She puts him down in the grass. He looks around and then at Saskia. She watches him. "Weird morning." she thinks. "How is this possible?" Little Bear strolls around the sandbox, finds a pebble and throws it in the air. Now and then he looks at Saskia. "Sometimes people think too much, like you are doing. Don't think so much. Are you having fun? Now?" "Yes." Saskia answers. "That is important.".Saskia doesn't know what else to say and she thinks: "I like it, now, it's exciting." "Good." Little Bear says. "But how is this all possible? It seems like a fairy-tale and I'm in it. Where did you come from? Magic only exists in stories, right? Who is Angelo? I like the now, but there is also later and before, right?" Saskia asks.

Bear tells about Bear

Little Bear starts telling about where he is from, about Angelo and the stars, and Saskia listens. "Now, before and later... Your phrased that really well, Saskia. People do, think and act a lot faster than when Angelo lived. They do, do, do and it's fun, fun, fun. They have schedules and agenda's... We have to do sports, go to clubs and music practice. Every day is filled up and that's good, but if you're not careful, you'll forget the here and now. There is always something that needs to be done and we are pushed more and more so the magic that surrounds us passes us by. That's a shame, don't you think? We're always thinking about later. We're always on the way to something new. That's a good thing, it keeps us feeling alive. If you're happy about the later, looking forward to it, you're happy with the now. But every now and again there has to be a break, otherwise we forget the now. Like we're here together in the grass; this is now, this is fun and nice, right? In Angelo's time, long ago, people used to think about what they were doing a lot more. They took their time for things and they only did them if it felt right. That made them happy so everything went better. So if you think about what you're doing and you feel good about it, you'll have more success. If something goes wrong, it's not wrong, it's just learning how it shóuldn't be and you start over. That way you don't see things as going wrong. You adjust, you learn and you carry on doing what you do, feeling everything is okay. Other people can be an example of what we want or don't want. You learn your own things your own way and the 'when' is up to you. Everything is good when you're happy about it and if you stay yourself. Follow your own road. Only you know what is best for you deep down, only you! It's important that you have fun on the way to something and that is what this summer holiday is about. If you know where you want to go and if you trust and believe in yourself, you'll always get there. I call it the magic." Little Bear looks at Saskia who has been listening to him. "Magic exists in fairy-tales, but it does exist around us as well. This is how it goes: you think about what you want and then it comes to you. Sometimes it may take a while, but it wíll come. Everything around you listens to you; the earth, sun, moon, stars and everything in between. It's all listening to you and it wants to give you what you desire. The magic means asking the right question and then to have faith. Sometimes it's an answer, sometimes it's something different and it can get to you in odd ways. I will tell you about Angelo, the man who made me.

His spot was near a river. He lived there alone in a small but cosy cottage with a fireplace he built himself to keep him warm in the winter. Angelo had found a fallen tree in the forest and he made an bench out of it. He used to sit there, on his bench, watching the river go by. All that water going towards unknown destinations, watching the trees on the other side rustle in the wind. Angelo felt very connected to everything around him when he sat there.

The sounds became more intense and he felt the wind like he was being touched by something invisible, blowing through his hair, against his clothes and stroking his face. Try sitting in the garden for a while without doing anything, just feel the wind. You'll feel amazing. Angelo heard things then he didn't hear when he was busy; the rustling of a mouse, the buzzing of a bee, all the different sounds of water like it was telling him where it was going. The scents of the woods and the flowers, new scents that surprised him. The feel of the wooden bench, his cottage behind him and then he knew he was made of the same things everything else was made of. Angelo felt that everything was good and he was happy. He did what was good for the earth and all living things. He knew the earth was good for him; everything came to him at the exact right moment. At the edge of the forest by the river was his beautiful world where you just picked an apple when you were hungry and walked to the river for a drink when you were thirsty. The forest was full of life. There were stags and does, goats, horses, rabbits, squirrels, all kinds of birds and sometimes a unicorn. There grew small, big and enormous trees. Those species are extinct now, they gave way to other things. The magic of

the forest was endless. There weren't many unicorns around, though, even then. They still exist, but they are very shy and can disguise themselves so that they are invisible. The same goes for gnomes, fairies and the slow giants. Now there are so many of us humans there's almost no space for them anymore. The giants, gnomes and fairies disappeared long ago to another realm, right next to ours. But like I said, everyone is being taken care of and everyone's questions are answered, so when the earth noticed there was no more room for them, she made this whole new world with a border that humans can't cross. It's like some kind of wall, but in some places the wall is thin and not many people live near it, so you can take a look inside sometimes. The more people there are, the thicker the wall.

In Angelo's time there was still just one realm.

A family of gnomes lived in a big oak tree nearby and the fairies lived in the forest giants, trees so big you can't even imagine. Humans, fairies and gnomes lived together in peace, but now they have their own realm and people can't see them anymore. Unless they really want to... If we find places where the wall is thin, or if we can make the wall a little thinner by ourselves. Angelo was very close to nature, something that is not common anymore for humans. The contact that gnomes and fairies have with mother earth is so strong that they are one. Because Angelo was so close with nature, the fairies saw him as a way too slow fairy. The gnomes saw him as a very happy, but really big gnome, and the slow giants saw him as a fast child. Angelo lived alone, but he wasn't lonely; he had a lot of visitors. Often he sat there quietly, thinking about why things were the way they were. Because Angelo thought so much, he knew a lot. He would ask a question in his head, become silent and just listen. If he listened carefully the answer would always come. If Angelo wasn't thinking, he was busy, making something or walking through the woods along the river. He was carefree. Sometimes he didn't do anything at all, just for the fun of it; just for doing nothing. Angelo loved everything and everyone, no matter what they looked like. All humans, animals, gnomes and fairies that lived around him loved Angelo in return. He was always happy and smiling, singing a song or playing a handcrafted flute. The animals would became curious and listened to him play. Sometimes a fairy came to watch as well, but the family of gnomes didn't like Angelo's music, and that's okay, because everyone likes different things. Angelo didn't really mind anyway because he was happy when he was playing the flute. That's what it's all about; doing what makes you happy. Often people came to him for advice when they needed it and he always tried to help them, he always had an answer. In fact, Angelo was kind of a celebrity, living on that beautiful young earth so long ago. He was warmed and cherished by that lovely sun, bathing in its fairy-tale-like glow. He was called 'wise Angelo', but more often 'happy Angelo', because he always was. Angelo woke up with a smile, happy a brand new day had started and wondering what it would bring him. Happily he did the things he wanted, sitting on his bench contentedly, watching everything around him, but also listening. He would listen for the answer after he had asked a question in his head. On clear nights he could watch the little lights that shone above him for hours. We now call them 'stars'. Angelo noticed that they all had their own place in the sky and their own movement. Did you ever notice that? Some of those stars were so lovely together that he remembered them and looked them up when they appeared at the sky. He even named them. Now we know those patterns are called 'constellations', but it was very clever of Angelo to know all that already then. He was also a craftsman who loved inventing and building things. Once he made a kite because he wanted to make something that flew like the birds and butterflies he saw. He made the kite out of twigs and leaves that he glued together with snailtrailslime. That was very sticky back then, but you don't have to try it now. It won't glue anything together, only make your hands slimy. The snails were twice as big as well, I don't think that anyone would like that. He got the rope for his kite from the spiders who kept his cottage bugfree for him. The spiders were a lot bigger then as well, so their threads were a lot stronger. Angelo didn't know any better, but I am sure most people wouldn't like bugs that big, especially moms!

When I was made by Angelo and living with him in that beautiful forest where people came to him with their questions, I learned a lot. If I don't know an answer, I ask him in my mind and then the answer always comes."

"Wow… Fairies, gnomes and unicorns… Really? Unbelievable! So…" Saskia whispers, "I can ask you anything?" "Yes," Little Bear says. After that long story he has to stretch his little legs a bit. He starts running through the grass, doing some somersaults. It's such a funny sight that Saskia shouts out in laughter.

The sun is shining, Little Bear and Saskia are lying at the bank of the stream, and it's nice and warm. Little Bear has a blade of grass in his mouth. Saskia asks: "I don't really understand, if I see nice things about mom, she becomes nicer herself?" "No," Little bear answers, "You see nice things but your mom doesn't become nicer because she was nice to begin with! Like I said: you get what you expect. At first you see your mother as always busy, busy, busy. You expect that she will be busy, so you séé her as busy all the time. But every day there are quiet moments too, but because you don't expect those, you don't see them. You're not around when they happen. This morning we switched that." "Little Bear, I can ask you anything, right? How is Hendrik? I'm worried about him, will he be okay?" "Worrying is expecting things to go wrong and that's not helping you, nor Hendrik. Worrying is never good. Hendrik has his own road to take, his own things to learn. His road is different from yours, as well as the things he has to learn." Silently Saskia thinks about this. "But will he be okay then?" "It's always going to be okay, because you can't do anything wrong." "Yeah, but he doesn't have a mom anymore and he might be held back a year. That's sad, isn't it?" "You're still worrying. I already told you not to do that." Little Bear smiles. "Yes, but…" Saskia says again. "Sometimes things are difficult to understand." Little Bear says. "But that's why I'm here." He takes the blade of grass from his mouth. "I will show you." He stands up straight and looks at Saskia. "Are you ready?" "Huh?" Saskia thinks and she watches Little Bear, being silent, his head tilted to one side as if he's trying to hear something only he can hear. Then he lifts up his paw and stardust swirls around him and then around Saskia as well, just like this morning. Saskia watches the twinkling in wonder…

The story of Smelly-feet Hendrik

Little Bear and Saskia are in the classroom. Remember that moment? Hendrik is in his seat with his head down. Most kids have already left the classroom, the last one is pushing his way through the door. It looks like they all want to start the summer holidays at once. When the last one has left, it's quiet. It looks and feels like a dream. Saskia is in the classroom and even though she can hear and see everything, she doesn't exactly know where she is. She sees Hendrik sitting there and the teacher standing near the whiteboard. I seems like Saskia is floating a little between the floor and the ceiling, watching them from above. Through the window she can see everyone on the playground. She watches the kids talk and laugh. Some show each other their report cards, others are already going home. Little Bear is on the bookcase, Saskia sees him point at the teacher. She watches her walk towards Hendrik and sit down on the table in front of him. She puts her finger under his chin and makes him look up. With eyes wide Hendrik looks at the teacher, waiting for what she's going to say. Hendrik is scared, Saskia can feel it, and then everything freezes. Just like in dreams everything is possible here. Little Bear walks on the shelf, watching the scene as well. The teacher is frozen, just like Hendrik and when Saskia looks outside she sees her classmate Jaap frozen mid-jump. "What does Hendrik expect?" Little Bear asks. "Hendrik is a thinker, just like you. He likes to draw; he makes beautiful drawings at home. He writes in his diary what he wishes, and he draws what that would look like. He uses the magic, like everyone else, without knowing it. He sends his expectations out into the world." Suddenly Saskia and Little Bear are somewhere else. Saskia sees a little room with a bed and a table against the wall, where Hendrik is writing in a notebook. He got the notebook from his mother before she died. Saskia knows this, but hów she knows it is unclear, just like in dreams. Hendrik is writing with a smile on his face. On the wall is a drawing that he just made; a woman, his mother, in beautiful colours between the clouds. Little Bear is on the table looking at Hendriks writing and then, suddenly, they are back in the classroom. Hendrik and the teacher are moving again, just like the leaves outside and Jaap finishes his jump.

"Although Hendrik expects to be held back a year, positive expectations are much stronger than negative ones. That's why the earth, sun, moon, stars and everything in between can't do anything else than bring what Hendrik expects, even though it might go differently than you would think…" Little Bear explains. "Hendrik," the teacher says, "The past schoolyear wasn't easy for you and your marks aren't high enough to let you pass." Tears start to form in Hendriks eyes. The teacher looks at him and wipes his tears away. Saskia sees a smile on her face that she has never seen before and it reminds her of how mom looked at her that morning. "But…" the teacher says slowly and Hendrik looks up. "I have talked to the principle. I made him a proposal and he agrees. For most of your subjects you're just one or two points short, but I know you can do it. So I want to help you this holiday and make sure you still pass every subject. That way you can pass just like everyone else, if you want to. Do you? We'll work every morning on the subjects you're having trouble with and we'll get there. What do you say?" Hendriks face lights up, like the sun comes out after the rain. He jumps up from his chair and leaps into the teachers arms. He hugs her as if he never wants to let go and Saskia sees the teacher wipe away a little tear herself. Suddenly Little Bear and Saskia are in Hendriks room again. It's night time and he is asleep. Saskia doesn't know how, but she can see his dream. Little Bear is at the foot of the bed and he's watching the tiny twinklings of stardust drift around the room. Saskia sees a woman walk out of the clouds; his mother. "The drawing!" she thinks, and she sees Hendrik walk towards the woman, who is looking healthy now. Saskia remembers her looking very ill. They talk, but Saskia can't hear what they say. "This is for Hendrik alone." Little Bear says. Suddenly they are lying at the bank of the stream again and stardust pulls back inside Little Bear. He picks up the blade of grass and puts it back in his mouth. He lays back down with his paws behind his head. "Do you see now that worrying doesn't help in the slightest? Things always turn out differently. Wish Hendrik all the best in the world and be kind to him, that will help him the most." Saskia is quiet, looking at the clouds floating by. She needs to process everything she saw, while Little Bear looks at her and follows her thoughts. She's trying to make sense of it all, she doesn't understand everything yet. Little Bear knows that it might take a while. It's quite something to suddenly have a talking teddy bear in your life and magic in a world so estranged from it. Little Bear thinks back on the time so long ago in a forest that doesn't exist anymore, living in the cottage with Angelo when magic was still normal.

Saskia and Little Bear lay there in the grass, warmed by the sun, both consumed by their own thoughts, while white clouds pass by. Saskia thinks about everything that has happened so far, but Little Bear thinks about Angelo and how he became Little Bear…

How Little Bear became Little Bear

One night Angelo was sitting on his bench. The sun was setting behind the trees on the other side of the river in lovely colours of yellow, orange, red and pink. Suddenly a big brown bear came out of the woods. It walked to the river and started fishing and playing in the water. Drops of water flew around, pearling in the soft fur. Angelo enjoyed watching that happy bear playing around and then he thought: "I want a bear! A bear for myself to pet and to play with, but a little smaller of course!" Angelo got excited by this idea and he made a little dance in the twilight. "Yes!" he called out. "I'm going to make a bear, I can do that!" In his mind's eye Angelo already saw how he could do it, how he could make the eyes, the fur, the paws and in his head the bear was already finished. The sun disappeared alongside the brown bear in the forest and slowly the moon came out. The lights appeared in the sky, the stars, and he enjoyed all that twinkling above him. Angelo told the stars about his idea to make a bear. He often talked to the stars and they always listened. He was tired, so he went inside and prepared to go to bed. He washed up and brushed his teeth. Toothbrushes like we know them didn't exist yet. He chewed on a twig until it became a brush and that's how he cleaned his teeth, because dentists didn't exist either. He used the leaves of sage for that, like his mother taught him. Happy about what the day had brought him, Angelo crawled into bed, but he couldn't fall asleep. He was so excited; he couldn't wait to get started on his bear! Thinking about how he would do it, Angelo eventually fell asleep and of course he dreamed about, you guessed it, a little bear.

The next day Angelo got up very early. He hadn't slept that much because he kept thinking of new things to make the bear. He was looking forward to start, rubbing and clapping his hands in glee. He looked outside and thought: "Oh my, it's still dark, I won't be able to find anything." He decided to have breakfast first. He ate an apple and put leaves in boiling water to make tea. Then he ate a slice of bread, made by a neighbour from across the hill, who always had a lot of questions and liked to trade bread for answers. Angelo also cracked a few hazelnuts and walnuts. Oh yeah, this is a good one. I want to tell you about this one: Angelo crushed the nuts, added honey and other things to put on his bread. I bet this sounds remarkably like Nutella hazelnutspread, but without the chocolate because cocoa hadn't been discovered yet. Slowly the sun started to rise so it was time to collect things, yay! Angelo found some dried grass in the woods to stuff the bear with. Then he started to look for something that could become eyes. On the riverbank he found two beautiful pebbles, so he took them with him. He was able to find everything effortlessly. Everywhere around him he saw things he could use and his imagination was endless.

Skipping merrily Angelo took all his materials home and started working. A belly, feet and arms, ears, eyes, everything sewn together with spider thread and snailtrailslime. Yes, that sounds disgusting, but it worked perfectly. Happily he sew things together, looked for new materials, and time flew by. Angelo was smiling and enjoying his craft, he forgot all about time. The snailtrailslime was sticking to his fingers and there was grass in his hair, but he didn't even notice. And then suddenly he was finished. It surprised him a little… He stood up, twigs and leaves falling to the floor, and he took two steps back to admire what he had made. There it was; a beautiful bear with everything a bear is supposed to have, because he had watched the big bear near the river closely. Angelo was pretty proud of what he had made. He couldn't believe his eyes, it was the first bear that was ever made on earth. He looked at it and it looked back with its shiny pebble-eyes. "Wow," Angelo thought, "It's so beautiful! Hello, bear." The bear didn't answer, it just stared at him. "Hello, bear," Angelo said again, but the bear still didn't answer. "Why isn't he talking back?" Angelo asked himself. He thought about it and the answer came in his head: 'because it's not alive.' "I am alive, but what does being alive even mean?" Angelo thought. "Why am I alive, and the big bear as well, but this little one isn't?" As usual one question draws out another. "Why are we alive? Why isn't this little bear alive too? I want it to be alive!" It was a difficult question and Angelo thought hard and long about it, for two days straight.

What happened during those two days that nobody knows

The 'that' that's always listening listened to Angelo. The earth, sun, moon, stars and everything in between and beyond whispered the answer in his ear. But what happened further was magic. Big Mister Bear and little Miss Bear are very high in the sky. You can see them if you want; when the nights sky is very clear and they're twinkling up there every night. They move very slowly, Angelo noticed. Now we call them 'stars' but back then people just called them 'lights' because they thought they were fireflies. They listened to Angelo and sent a piece of star towards Little Bear. Angelo didn't see that and neither did Little Bear, because you can't see with riverpebble-eyes. Some people did see it though. They looked up and saw two falling stars, so they made a wish. People did that, even then, and all their wishes came true. The two stars fell all the way to earth, right towards the cottage of Angelo and Little Bear. Through the forest they danced around each other, twinkling merrily, making happy little sounds and startling animals, gnomes and fairies. Eventually they swirled around the cottage and around the head of the soundly asleep Angelo, who didn't notice anything. And then… they disappeared right into Little Bear!

Angelo discovers Little Bear

Angelo woke up and rubbed his eyes. He got out of bed, stretching, while Little Bear was watching him. "Good morning, Angelo." he said. Angelo yelped, tripped and fell over. "Do be careful!" Little Bear said grinning. "What… How… Huh… I… You…" Angelo stammered. He fell silent and looked at Little Bear who was watching him with his little riverstone eyes. They were glistening full of life now. Little Bear was laughing at Angelo, sitting there on the floor amazed with huge eyes and his mouth slightly open. "Sit down for a moment." Little Bear said, gesturing to a chair. Angelo scrambled up and took a seat. "But… how?" he muttered. Little Bear smiled and said: "You know how it works by now. Everyone gets what he thinks about most. You asked and you let go. You trusted and you're happy, so here I am. Your wish is granted. I'm here and my name is Little Bear." When Angelo calmed down a bit and found his voice again, he started asking Little Bear a lot of questions. Where he came from, and all kinds of other things, and he tickled his tummy. This was after a while of course, because Angelo didn't dare to at first. Little Bear used to feel cold, but now he was warm. "Stop!" Little Bear shouted, giggling, "That tickles!" and he rolled around laughing. Angelo and Little Bear danced around the tiny cottage. Little Bear asked Angelo a lot of questions as well, like: "Where am I?" and "What's it called here?" They talked together all day and well into the night. When they were sitting outside on the bench, tired from all the talking, they looked up at the stars. Two constellations were shining extra bright that night. "That's where I'm from, Angelo." Little Bear said, "I don't know how, but I can feel it when I look at them, I know it." A while later they fell asleep together on the bench in front of Angelo's cottage. That was the start of a whole new life for Angelo and Little Bear. They became friends for life. This is how Little Bear started his life on earth, made by the wise and happy Angelo, who lived so long ago, plus a little magic.

That magic is all everywhere around you. When you're happy, you can see it, when you're quiet, you can feel it and when you listen, you can hear it. It's just as strong as when Angelo lived by the river together with Little Bear. Angelo taught him everything, so he knows just as much, but because the stars inside him always helped him, he was able to listen even better. Big Mister Bear and Little Miss Bear are still there as well. You can see them if you look at the sky on a clear night. And sometimes Little Bear appears. To whom? This time to Saskia.

The day continues

Dad is walking through the garden carrying a bag of hay and a shovel to clean Pluisjes home. Saskia is holding Pluisje, his little nose going up and down, smelling all the new scents. Little Bear is sitting on the rabbit home, watching dad cleaning it and making a cosy home again for Pluis. To dad he looks like an old teddy bear with some rips and holes, but Saskia smiles, watching the beautiful bear walking around the roof. He's looking over the edge every now and then to see how it's going. Then he pinches his nose when dad removes the triangle of droppings and he jumps backwards. Only Saskia can see that. When everything is ready, she puts Pluisje back in his home.

She, dad and Little Bear watch him in his clean home, jumping from left to right, flattening the hay, making a cosy nest in the corner. Then he stops when he smells the lettuce dad got from mom to feed him. Pluisje starts eating it, first things first. When dad heads back inside, Little Bear asks Saskia: "Can you show me where you play and have fun? I've never been here, on this place on earth. Show me the people and their houses. I want to see how they live." Saskia takes Little Bear in her arms and strolls out of the garden.

The village, Barking Dog and Rugged Cees

Together they walk through the little streets and alleys. Saskia tells Little Bear about the village and its inhabitants. Little Bear is quiet, listening to her and watching everything. The sun is warm, white clouds drift by as they look out over the fields at the edge of the village. Rugged Cees' goat is bleating nearby. They look over and see it standing on the roof of its wooden house with his goatee sticking out. The goat bleats loudly to Saskia and Little Bear. They walk towards the house where all kinds of junk is lying in the garden, paint is coming down from the window frames and the gutter came off. It's lying on the ground now with dandelions growing in it. It kind of looks like a very long flowerpot. Rugged Cees lives here with Barking Dog, the dog without a real name. Barking Dog is standing next to the house. He is quiet and that is quite unusual. Barking Dog is watching Saskia and Little Bear with his ears upright and his tail frozen mid wag. "Why is he afraid of everyone and why is he always barking?" Saskia asks. "He is scared and insecure because he had a bad youth. He's afraid that will return, every day." Little Bear answers. "But he's okay now, isn't he?" "Yes, but he learned the wrong things and now he can't change anymore. Some people experience that as well. He thinks about bad things, so he asks bad things and then bad things come." Little Bear explains. "But with me he isn't scared." Saskia says. "Nor with me. He can see me like you do, just as I am, and he can feel a lot more than people can. He feels safe with us, so the dog he once was comes out." Barking Dog listens, his head tilted one way and then the other. He sees Saskia with a little animal on her arm. He is happy, he's feeling good, so he wags his tail. "Sweet masters, kind masters to play with!" Dog thinks. He runs off to find the ball he was playing with that morning with Big Master. Big Master had to leave with another master. That one comes around often, but Barking Dog is afraid of him because he has a dark cloud around him. All masters have such a cloud, but that little master doesn't and neither does the thing on her arm. His nose quickly finds the ball and a few seconds later he drops it at Saskia's feet. He barks and starts jumping up and down: he wants to play! Saskia picks up the ball, while Barking Dog is looking up at her expectantly. She throws the ball as far as possible and he runs off to retrieve it. Saskia, Little Bear and Barking Dog spend a while playing like that. Later they are sitting against an apple tree with the dog lying on the ground, tired from playing, content and happy. The goat is lying in his home on fresh hay in a garden full of junk. "Why is Cees so weird and why do people fear him?" Saskia asks softly. Little Bear looks at Saskia and the dog, lying there so relaxed. When he looks inside the dogs mind, he sees his thoughts. It makes him happy, because Dog is happy right now, as he should be. The bad memories are further away than they usually are. Carefully he uses a little magic to push them even further away. Small twinklings sparkle around the dogs head. The bad memories are even deeper buried and that will improve his life a bit more. Dog stretches and looks at Little Bear, his eyes big and full of trust. "Rugged Cees is a little bit like Barking Dog. He experiences bad things and he has bad memories, so that made him who he is now. He's not weird; that's just your opinion. He's just Cees, nothing more and nothing less and he is okay the way he is. It's your judgement of him and that of others. When someone does things in a different way, it's often misunderstood and seen as weird. Cees grew up without parents; he is an orphan and he experienced very little love, so he is not expecting it anymore. That's why he won't get it anymore. That is the law; you always get what you want and ask for. You receive what you pay attention to." "That's not fair!" Saskia says loudly. "Yes, it is. The earth, sun, moon, stars and everything in between can't control or live your life for you. Thát would be unfair. Everyone must make their own choices and walk their own paths. You think and ask, so be aware of what you think about and aware of what you ask." Saskia is quiet and thinks about everything Little Bear has told her.

She understand, but she doesn't at the same time. It's like she can't quite grasp it. She scoots over a little bit and lies down on her back on a patch of grass the goat didn't eat yet. She looks through the leaves of the apple tree to the white clouds that slowly drift closer. When she stops thinking about it, it gets more clear. Little Bear listens to her thoughts contentedly. Far away he sees Rugged Cees strolling on the road towards his house. We wouldn't be able to see that, Cees is too far away, but Little Bear can do a lot more than we can. Cees brought his pony to the farm of Farmer Jan. There he will have a lot more room to run. The pony knew where he was going and he expected the grass and the running. In a certain way that makes Cees happy as well. That is usually different, Little Bear notices when he listens to Cees' thoughts. He doesn't always understand other people that well, why they do what they do. He mostly think's it's him, so that's why Barking Dog found him; they are alike. Little Bear doesn't go into Cees' thoughts too deep because he is here for Saskia. He wouldn't even be able to make contact with Cees, he is too far away from the magic. Little Bear let's go of Rugged Cees's mind, enlarges the world he cán see, and then he notices by the twinkling in his belly that it is time to leave Saskia. He's being called by another child in another place for a new adventure.

Little Bear says goodbye

"Saskia," Little Bear says, "Saskia, listen carefully. I have got to go. I'm being called, we have to say goodbye." With big eyes Saskia looks at Little Bear. "But why…" she stammers, "Why?" "Another child is calling me, is asking…" Saskia sees that Little Bears eyes are looking at something she cannot see, something far, very far away. Little Bear is looking at another place in the world in a way we can't anymore, we have forgotten how to. We can learn again to see the world again that way, though.

Little Bear sees a boy, Danny is his name, walking through a forest. It's still spring, the leaves have just appeared on the trees, al fresh and green. Some trees are still waiting, slumbering and empty. The morning sun is shining through the canopy, just awake and risen. Danny is sad and alone. Behind his house are the woods and a little walk away is a small lake. On a spot nobody knows about there is a big round rock that Danny sits down on. Little Bear sees him sitting there with the sun playing in the treetops. The boy is mad at himself. He has to go to the hospital today and he doesn't want to. Little Bear looks inside Danny's mind and he sees his thought. Danny is sitting there often, by that quiet water, thinking and asking his questions. The magic is calling Little Bear to him. "I'm coming," Little Bear says, "Have patience…" Danny looks up surprised. Did he hear something?

"Little Bear, you have to stay with me, forever!" Saskia shouts, but Little Bear doesn't hear her now.

He is watching and listening. Little stars are swirling around him and he is bathing in a beautiful light. He seems to be growing, Saskia can see Little Bear change. "Bye, Saskia, bye sweet, sweet Saskia…" Saskia is holding Little Bear in her arms now and keeps on whispering: "Stay with me…" She is crying. "Stop." Little Bear says, "Don't be sad. I'm not far away." Light and tiny stars exit and enter Little Bear and swirl around him and Saskia. "I'm going to Danny now, but I'll never forget you, Saskia." Little Bear starts floating away from her, further and further. "Bye, sweet Saskia!" Little Bear sends some magic towards her to show her where he is going. He also shows her in a flash everything they did together; a tiny moment in which time is pressed together like only magic can do. Suddenly Saskia understands what Little Bear has to do and why, and she is happy he will be helping Danny now. Slowly Little Bear floats away, all the way up to the white clouds where he disappears into a big white one. It transforms into Little Bear, huge and woolly with a big smile on his bear face and waving his paw. "Bye, Little Bear, bye beautiful, sweet Little Bear! See you! Say hi to Danny from me!" Saskia shouts as the wind scatters the cloud… And then he's gone.

Saskia gets up and walks out of Rugged Cees' garden with a tear rolling down her cheek. She's going home, to mom. Suddenly she hears the voice of Little Bear inside her mind. "I'll always be here, you only have to think of me…" Saskia knows it's true and she wipes the tear away. She looks around to see the beautiful flowers and trees and she smiles. "Bye, Little Bear, see you later." Happy, smiling and crying at the same time she walks through the streets. Little Bear is no longer with her, he is gone, but he's still close because it's like she

can hear him in her mind. Saskia now knows how that works, Little Bear taught her. It's like the whole world changed; magic is whispering in her thoughts.

"Hi, Saskia!" Smelly-feet Hendrik is in the playground on the swings. He has a big smile on his face that Saskia has never seen before.

"Hi, Hendrik! Want to play here together tomorrow?" "Sure!" Hendrik answers happily. "I can be here around one o clock, is that okay?" Saskia asks. Hendrik nods. "See you tomorrow then!" Saskia waves to him once and then she walks home, smiling to herself.

"Hi mom!" Mom is planting flowers in the garden. "Hi, Sas," she says, "How are you, sweetie?" "I'm great! Can I help you?" "That would be lovely." mom says surprised, watching her daughter. "Saskia changed today," she thinks and then she's startled when Saskia kisses her firmly on the cheek. "Huh!" "I'm getting those red flowers, I want to plant them over there. Is that okay, mom?" Saskia laughs, seeing her mother kneeling there, wearing dads way too large gardening gloves, her mouth slightly open in surprise. "Come on, mom, carry on, this way we'll never be finished." They look at each other, burst out laughing and start to roll around in the grass together. Little Bear watches them and smiles.

The end.

About the Authors

Ben and Annelies [BoAnn] are a Dutch couple with two lovely daughters and a beautiful grandson, living in the Netherlands. They were married for 19 years when they separated. Two years later they found each other again and they both had grown much stronger and wiser because of the separation. They are artists: Ben as a writer, a craftsman and a pencil-artist, and Annelies in art-painting. They want to be a light to the world in their unique way. Along the way they came across Louise Hay and later on the teachings of Abraham Hicks. Together they grew even stronger and they found peace and wisdom in these teachings. They found them such great teachers, that they got the inspiration to write this book. It's about children and the wisdom of a little bear, who teaches the children about the Universe and their daily problems, and how to go about it so they can live happily ever after. The children are the future! In their way Ben and Annelies would like to be a little guiding light to make better generations, where there is more love, respect and understanding for each other and nature.

This first book of the series; "The Magic of Little Bear" is their debut. Ben and Annelies hope you like it, so they can write many more.

Thank you for helping them by buying this book!
They wish you a great journey and life!
For the artwork of Annelies you can visit:
www.studioann.nl.

This book is edited and translated by Perla Schippers-Anröchte.

Printed in the United States
By Bookmasters